Published by B & F Publishing, Spokane, Washington

Developed in Post Falls, Idaho by Crown Media and Printing, Inc.
www.crownmediacorp.com

ISBN# 978-1-4507-3351-9

Cougar Cub Tales
I'm Just Like You

Written and Illustrated by
Sharon Cramer

Dedicated to Cole, Shad and Chase

The cougar cub kittens were sister and brother.

They lived in their den, just one and the other,

For in a terrible snow... long ago...

They had lost their dear mother.

The cubs both ran into the forest to play

For it was a most MAGNIFULOUS day!

There were castles to scale

And dragons to slay.

They imagined all sorts of marvelous things,

Like glow-in-dark fur, and two sets of wings.

They scaled and they flew...

...They colored and drew,

And found sparkly treasures, jewels and rings!

When suddenly just as their fur was a-glowing...

And wings were a-flapping, all to-ing and fro-ing,

They spied such a creature, beyond the compare!

All boy cougar did was to stop and to stare...

The girl cougar whispered, just a bit smug,

"Why THAT doesn't look like a REAL cougar cub..."

But the creature, he sported some very fine ears.

He quickly retorted, "How wrong to have fears...

For I am a cougar-cub, sure as can be...

...Ask me a cougar-cub question... you'll see."

"You don't have a tail," the boy cougar said.

The creature replied with a shake of his head,

"Oh yes, but I do, it's just I can't catch it...

But... Neither can you!"

And they each tried in vain till their faces were blue!

The cougar cubs laughed,

At once charmed by the game.

But they still weren't convinced

That they were the same.

The girl cougar ventured, "Your ears are too big."

The boy cougar nodded, "Too big and too hairy."

Their new friend responded,

"It makes me more merry...

And so much more able to hear something SCARY!"

"For I would hope I don't hear better than you,

When the Ziggly-Zort monster...

...Escapes from the zoo!"

"Oh No!" the cubs cried,

"We both hear quite well!"

And it was agreed that ALL ears are swell...

"You're covered with spots...

From your head to your toes,

Your knuckles and knees...

Your tail and your nose!"

"Oh… Why one day they fell, like the stars from the sky,

And covered my fur in the blink of an eye.

And any day now, it could happen to you!

It's rare… but the stars just might cover you too!"

"Oh I want some star spots on my fur as well!"

The girl cougar shouted and jumped up and down.

"It may happen... just when, you never can tell...

...Or stripes, that circle you round and around!"

"But your eyes," the cubs noticed

As day turned to night,

"We don't think you see as well as one might."

And then they were sorry they said such a thing,

But the little cub nodded and started to sing,

"Let me lead you both home, for my feet know the trail.

My heart is my eyes, and my friends it won't fail."

And on through the dark the cubs followed his... TAIL!

The forest was tangled with shadows by then

As back through the stickety wicket they followed.

Over the river and back through the glen,

Up the black mountain and down through the hollow...

Till all of a sudden such a wonderlous sight.

There in the distance, just to the right...

Lay their home, and the cubs cheered with delight!

And finally safe once again at the den

The cougar cubs realized they had a new friend,

And perhaps... just perhaps...

He really WAS just like them.

The End

Sharon Jean Cramer was born in Jamestown, New York in 1960. She has lived throughout the United States, finally settling in the Pacific Northwest. She went to Idaho State University and then Gonzaga University. She is married and has three sons of her own. She and the cougar cubs currently reside, happily, in Spokane, Washington.

Other books by Sharon Cramer:
• Cougar Cub Tales: Lost and Alone
• Cougar Cub Tales: The Sneezy Wheezy Day

Child labor was not used in the production of this book.
B & F Publishing and Crown Media & Printing, Inc print the Cougar Cub Tales in an ISO 9001 certified workplace that has been approved by the BSCI (Business Social Compliance Initiative)